Based on the screenplay "Pups Turn On the Lights"
by Scott Albert

Illustrated by Fabrizio Petrossi

A GOLDEN BOOK • NEW YORK

T#: 314098
randomhousekids.com
ISBN 978-0-553-52277-8
Printed in the United States of America
10 9 8 7 6 5 4 3 2 1

One windy afternoon in Adventure Bay, a box moved down the street toward Katie's Pet Parlor. But this box wasn't being blown by the wind. *It was creeping down the street on eight paws!*

Suddenly, a big gust blew the box away, revealing Skye and Rubble underneath. They quickly scampered into the shop.

Inside, Ryder, Katie, and Rocky were getting ready for Chase's surprise birthday party.

"Who's making sure Chase doesn't surprise *us* while we set up?" Skye asked.

"Marshall," Rocky said. "He can keep a secret—can't he?"

Across town, Marshall and Chase were playing in Pup Park. They swung on the swings and slid down the slide.

"Maybe we should go find Ryder and the pups," Chase said.

"No!" Marshall protested. "We can't! Because it's, um, so nice out."

Just then, the wind picked up again and blew them right across the park!

Back at the Pet Parlor, the lights suddenly went dark, and Katie's mixer stopped.

"All the lights on the street are out!" Rocky yelped.

Ryder thought he knew what was wrong. "PAW Patrol, to the Lookout!"

The team raced to the Lookout. But without
electricity, the doors wouldn't open. Luckily,
Rocky had a screwdriver, which did the trick.

Once they were inside, Ryder used his telescope to check Adventure Bay's windmills. "Just as I thought," he said. "The wind broke a propeller. Since the windmill can't turn, it can't make electricity. We need to fix it!"

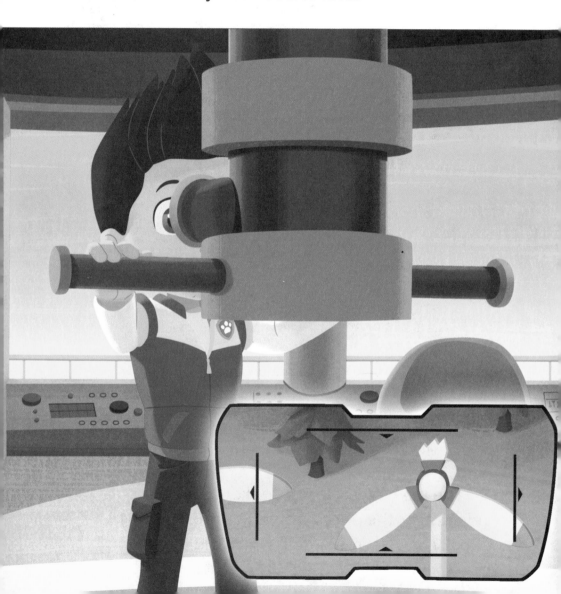

Ryder looked at Rocky. "We'll need something from your truck to fix the broken blade."

"Green means go!" Rocky said, preparing for action.

"We'll need Marshall's ladder to climb up and fix the windmill," said Ryder.

Marshall nodded. "I'm fired up!"

"Chase, the traffic lights won't work without electricity," Ryder continued. "I need you to use your siren and megaphone to direct traffic."

"These paws uphold the laws," Chase declared.

Meanwhile, Skye, Zuma, and Rubble raced back to the Pet Parlor to continue setting up for Chase's surprise party. It was very dark, but Katie had a flashlight.

At the center of town, Chase busily directed traffic.
"You're our hero," Mayor Goodway said as she
crossed the street safely.
"I'm just doing my PAW Patrol duty," Chase said.

Up in the hills, Ryder, Marshall, and Rocky went to work on the broken windmill. Ryder climbed Marshall's ladder and removed the old blade while Rocky looked for a replacement piece.

"No, not a tire . . . not a lawn chair," Rocky said, pulling stuff out of his truck. At last he found what he wanted. "Here it is—my old surfboard!

"This surfboard will catch a breeze and help turn it into electricity," Rocky said as he bolted the board into place. The wind picked up and the windmill started to turn. Lights came on all over Adventure Bay!

The traffic lights started working again.
"Ryder and the PAW Patrol did it!" Chase
announced through his megaphone. "My work
here is done!"

The lights in the Pet Parlor glowed brightly.
"Hooray!" cheered Skye, but then she
frowned. "Aw! There's no time to make a cake."
Katie thought for a moment. "I have an idea!"

As Chase drove back to the Lookout, he got a call from Ryder. "We need you at Katie's— in a hurry!"

When Chase got there, everything was dark and quiet.

Chase stepped inside. The lights went on.
"SURPRISE!" everyone yelled.

Chase was amazed. "Wow! You guys turned
the lights back on AND made a party for me?"

"We didn't have time to bake you a real cake," Katie
said, "so we hope you like your pup-treat cookie cake."

"Whenever it's your birthday, just yelp for help!" Ryder said with a laugh. All the puppies cheered and enjoyed a taste of Chase's special cake.